Fact Cat

FORCES AND MAGNETS

Sonya Newland

WAYLAND
www.waylandbooks.co.uk

FACT CAT

Get your paws on this fantastic new mega-series from Wayland!

Join our Fact Cat on a journey of fun learning about every subject under the sun!

First published in Great Britain in 2017 by Wayland
Copyright © Hodder and Stoughton Limited, 2017

ISBN: 978 1 5263 0172 7

10 9 8 7 6 5 4 3 2 1

MIX
Paper from responsible sources
FSC® C104740

Wayland
An imprint of Hachette Children's Group
Part of Hodder & Stough[...]
Carmelite House
50 Victoria Embankment
London EC4Y 0DZ

An Hachette UK Compan[...]
www.hachette.co.uk
www.hachettechildrens.[...]

A catalogue for this title[...]
the British Library
Printed and bound in Ch[...]

Produced for Wayland by
White-Thomson Publishing Ltd
www.wtpub.co.uk

Editor: Sonya Newland
Design: Clare Nicholas
Fact Cat illustrations: Shutterstock/Julien Troneur
Consultant: Karina Philip

Picture and illustration credits:
iStock: Tatomm 4tr, 0871540 BC LTD. 4bl, 8 micut, tomch 10, VisualCommunications 12, JackF 15, PKM1 17b, Matthew Cole 19; NASA: 13; Shutterstock: Rob Hyrons 4tl, Janis Smits 4br, Darren Baker 5, Air Images 6, Mino Surkala 7, IM_photo 9, Microgen 11, Lisa Steyn 14tl, Lorena Fernandez 14tm, nanantachoke 14tr, RomanR 14bl, Costin Constantinescu 14 br, MilanB 16l, Jan H. Andersen 16r, AngelPet 17t, NoPainNoGain 18, Snowbelle 20, Christopher Wood 21l, ILYA AKINSHIN 21r.

The author, Sonya Newland, is a writer and editor specialising in children's educational publishing.

The consultant, Karina Philip, is a teacher and a primary literacy consultant with an MA in creative writing.

FACT CAT FACT

There is a question for you to answer on every spread in this book. You can check your answers on page 24.

CONTENTS

WHAT ARE FORCES?

A force is a push or a pull. Forces are at work all around you. You cannot see them, but you can see the effect they have on things.

Stretching, squashing and bending are all forces. What is the force in the fourth picture?

stretching

squashing

bending

Forces can be strong or weak. A strong push on a swing will make it go faster and higher than a weak push.

FACT CAT FACT

Forces even work inside your body. Your **muscles** pull on your **bones** to make you move.

HOW FORCES WORK

Forces affect objects in different ways. Pulling on your dog's lead will make him slow down. Pushing a toy car will make it speed up or change **direction**.

Forces can change the shape of objects. When the girl sits on the space hopper, her weight pushes down and squashes it.

Forces work in pairs. If the forces are the same size, they cancel each other out. This means they do not change the way an object moves.

If one force is bigger than another, an object will start moving or get faster.

FACT CAT FACT

Forces are measured in units called **newtons**. Who are they named after?

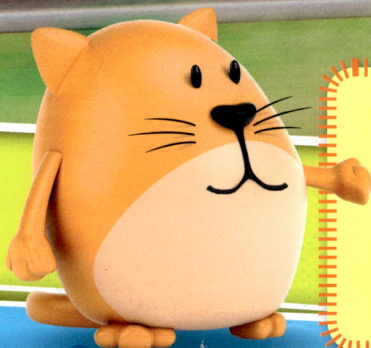

FRICTION

Friction happens when two objects rub against each other. It always slows the objects down. Friction between your feet and the pavement stops you slipping over.

To **increase** friction, trainers have patterns in the **sole**. These grip the ground firmly when you walk or run.

Rough **surfaces** like gravel or sandpaper create more friction than smooth surfaces. It is harder to push something along a carpet than a wooden floor.

The smooth surface of snow creates hardly any friction, so it is good for skiing and sledging.

FACT CAT FACT

Friction also creates heat. What happens if you rub your hands together?

AIR RESISTANCE

Air resistance is a type of friction. It affects objects that are flying or falling. A lot of air resistance makes something fall more slowly.

As this parachute falls towards Earth, air resistance slows it down. Which direction does air resistance push?

Streamlined shapes **reduce** air resistance. Air flows more easily over long, thin shapes and smooth surfaces.

When you swim, you can feel the force of the water pushing against you. This is a type of friction called **water resistance**.

FACT CAT FACT

There is no air resistance in space because there is no air beyond Earth.

GRAVITY

All the things you see around you are held on Earth by **gravity**. Gravity pulls things together. Big, heavy objects have stronger gravity than lighter ones.

This bungee jumper falls downwards when he jumps because Earth's strong gravity pulls everything towards it.

Earth's gravity pulls on the Moon to keep it in **orbit**. The pull of gravity between the planets and the Sun keeps the **Solar System** moving.

There is no gravity out in space. What would happen if this **astronaut** was not connected to the spacecraft?

FACT CAT FACT

The rise and fall of the **tides** are caused by the gravity of the Sun and the Moon pulling on the sea.

WHAT ARE MAGNETS?

A magnet is anything that attracts **magnetic** objects. Most materials are not magnetic. For example, magnets do not attract paper, glass, wood or plastic.

We use different materials to make different things. Which of these objects are magnetic?

Most **metals** are magnetic, but not all of them are. Metals such as aluminium and copper are not magnetic.

This pan and ladle are made of steel. They are magnetic because steel is made mostly from iron.

FACT CAT FACT

Most forces affect objects only when they touch them. Gravity and **magnetism** affect objects without touching them.

TYPES OF MAGNET

Magnets come in many different shapes and sizes. For science experiments, you might use a **bar magnet** or a **horseshoe magnet**.

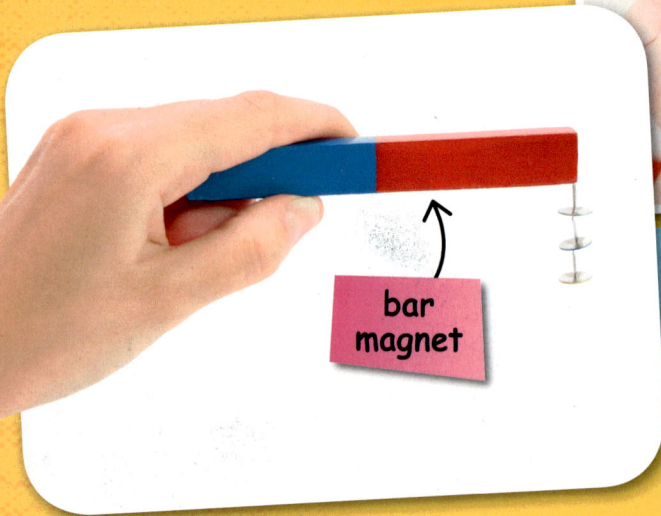

horseshoe magnet

bar magnet

Bar magnets and horseshoe magnets are two types. What is another type of magnet you might use at school?

FACT CAT FACT

The force of a magnet gets stronger the closer an object is to it.

Large magnets like this are strong enough to pick up big pieces of scrap metal.

Magnets are also used in computers and televisions.

Some roller coasters use magnets to get them started and help them slow down at the end of the ride.

NORTH AND SOUTH POLES

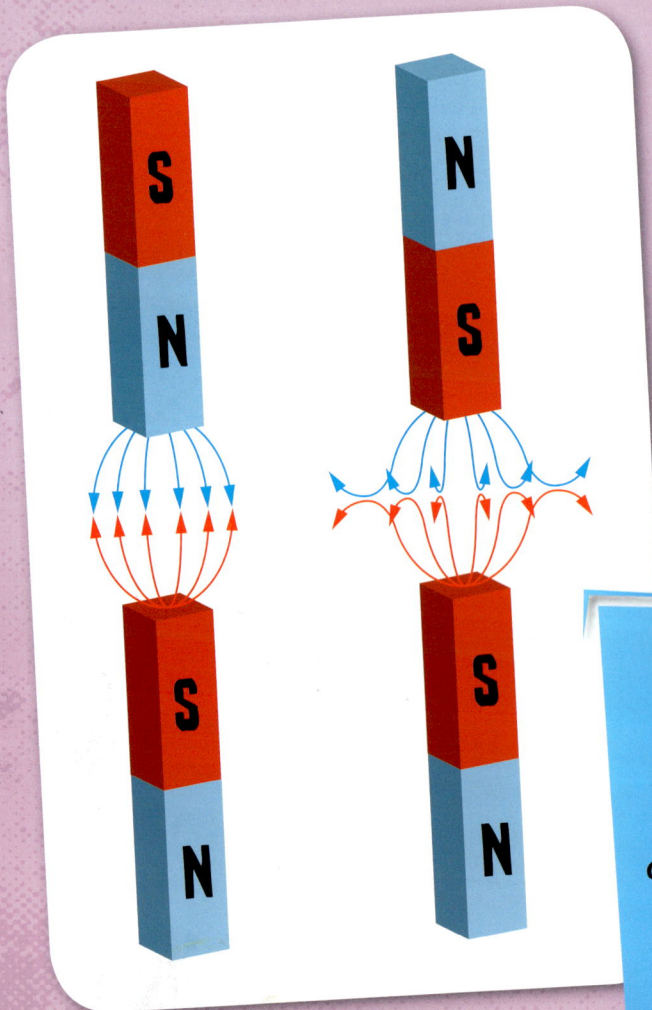

All magnets have a north pole and a south pole. Opposite poles **attract** each other. Two north poles or two south poles **repel** each other.

The north poles of these magnets are blue and the south poles are red. The arrows show how they pull together or push away.

This magnetic force comes from the poles. Outside the magnet, the force travels from the north pole to the south pole. Inside the magnet, it travels back from south to north.

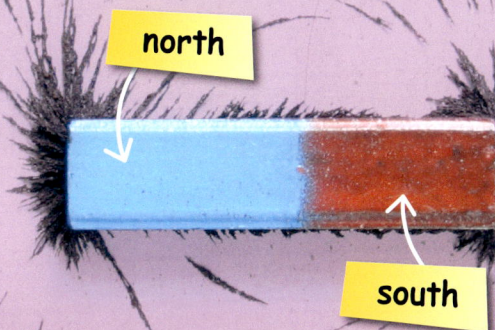

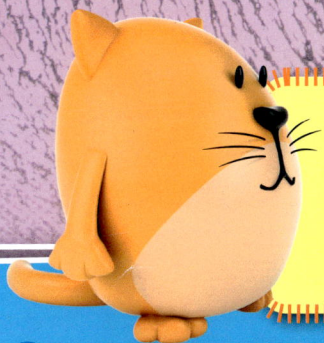

north

south

FACT CAT FACT

A **force field** is the area around a magnet that affects objects.

MAGNETIC EARTH

Earth is like a giant magnet. In the middle of Earth is a ball made of metal. This creates a huge magnetic force field around Earth as the planet spins.

Earth's magnetic field is the same shape as the magnetic field of a bar magnet (see page 19).

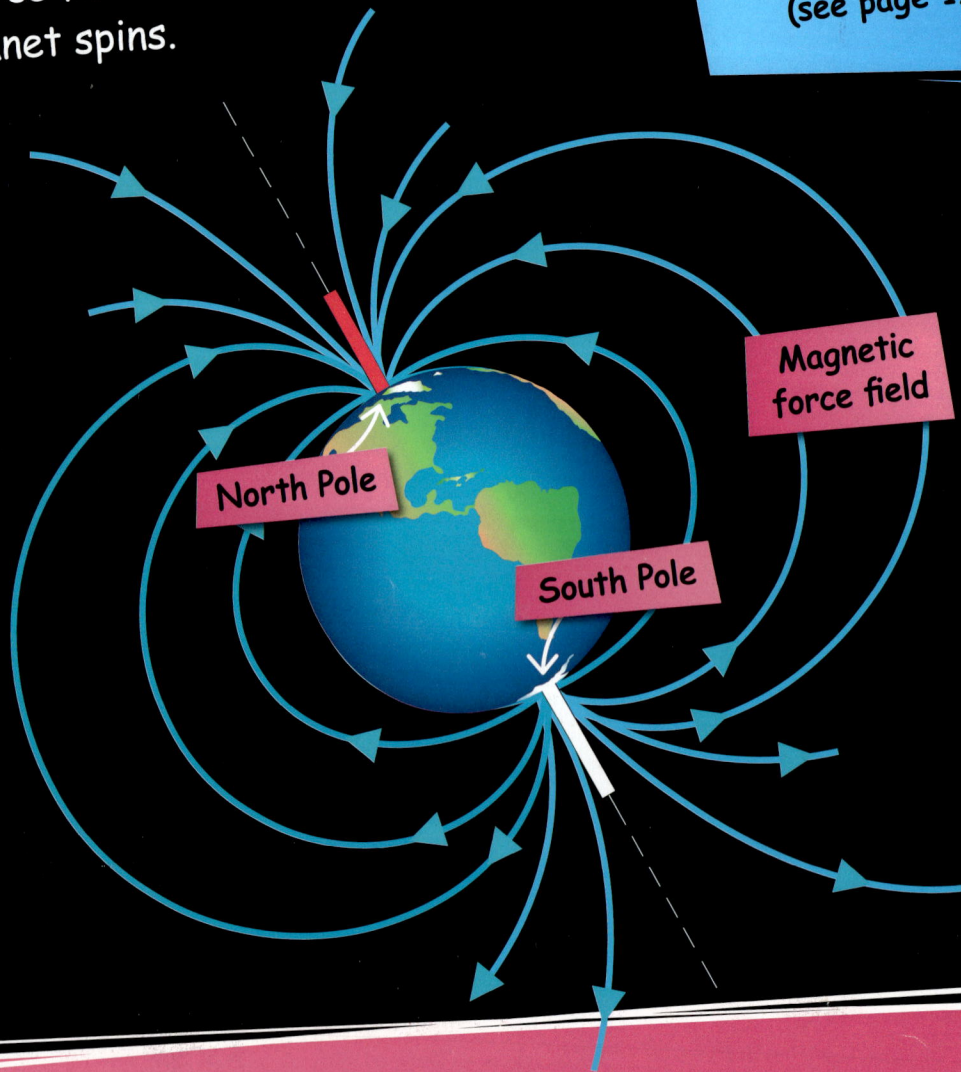

Magnetic force field

North Pole

South Pole

Magnets on Earth are affected by its magnetic field. A magnet that can move freely will turn so that one end points towards the North Pole and the other towards the South Pole.

FACT CAT FACT

Earth's magnetic field stretches nearly 60,000 km into space. That's one-fifth of the way to the Moon!

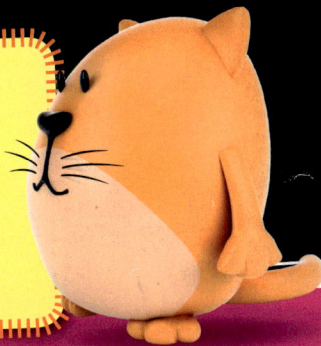

QUIZ

Try to answer the questions below. Look back through the book to help you. Check your answers on page 24.

1 What units do we use to measure forces?

a) newtons

b) kilograms

c) centimetres

2 Smooth surfaces create more friction than rough surfaces. True or not true?

a) true

b) not true

3 Which force stops things on Earth floating off into space?

a) friction

b) gravity

c) air resistance

4 All metals are magnetic. True or not true?

a) true

b) not true

5 The north pole of one magnet attracts the south pole of another magnet. True or not true?

a) true

b) not true

6 What type of force is caused by Earth's metal core?

a) magnetism

b) gravity

c) friction

GLOSSARY

air resistance friction between an object and air

astronaut someone who goes into space

attract pull together

bar magnet a long, straight magnet, with poles at each end

bones the hard pieces that make up the solid frame of the body

compass a device that helps people travel in the right direction

direction the path that something moves along or the place it points to

force field the area where a force is at work

friction the force between two objects that are rubbing against each other

gravity a force that pulls objects together

horseshoe magnet a curved magnet, whose poles are close together

increase make bigger

magnetic something that is attracted to a magnet

magnetism the force that acts on magnetic materials

metals hard, shiny substances

muscles parts of the body attached to bones that stretch or shrink to make you move

newtons the units used to measure forces

orbit the path that objects in space move in around other objects

reduce make smaller

repel push apart

Solar System the planets, including Earth, that move around the Sun

sole the bottom of a shoe

streamlined something that is specially shaped so that air or water can move over it easily

surface the outside layer of something

tides the rise and fall of the sea throughout the day

water resistance friction between an object and water

INDEX

ANSWERS

Pages 4–21

Page 4: Twisting

Page 7: The scientist Sir Isaac Newton

Page 9: They get warmer

Page 10: Upwards

Page 12: He would float off into space

Page 13: The paperclips and the nails

Page 16: A ring magnet or a button magnet

Page 19: At the poles

Page 21: North, South, East and West

Quiz answers

1   a – newtons

2   not true – rough surfaces create more friction

3   b – gravity

4   not true – most metals are magnetic, but not all

5   true

6   a – magnetism

OTHER TITLES IN THE FACT CAT SERIES...

WAYLAND
www.waylandbooks.co.uk